Scribner

An Imprint of Simon & Schuster, Inc.

1230 Avenue of the Americas

New York, NY 10020

Adapted from *The Great Gatsby* by F. Scott Fitzgerald

Copyright © 1925 by Charles Scribner's Sons

Copyright renewed 1953 by Frances Scott Fitzgerald Lanahan

Adapted Text and Illustration copyright © 2020 by Simon & Schuster, Inc.

First Scribner trade paperback edition June 2020

SCRIBNER and design are registered trademarks of The Gale Group, Inc., used under license
by Simon & Schuster, Inc., the publisher of this work.

For information about special discounts for bulk purchases,
please contact Simon & Schuster Special Sales
at 1-866-506-1949 or business@simonandschuster.com.

The Simon & Schuster Speakers Bureau can bring authors to your live event.
For more information or to book an event, contact the Simon & Schuster Speakers
Bureau at 1-866-248-3049 or visit our website at www.simonspeakers.com.

Manufactured in the United States of America

3   5   7   9   10   8   6   4   2

Library of Congress Cataloging-in-Publication Data has been applied for.

ISBN 978-1-9821-4452-4
ISBN 978-1-9821-4454-8 (pbk)
ISBN 978-1-9821-4453-1 (ebook)

THE GREAT GATSBY

F. Scott Fitzgerald

THE GRAPHIC NOVEL

Illustrated by Aya Morton

Text adapted by Fred Fordham

SCRIBNER

New York   London   Toronto   Sydney   New Delhi

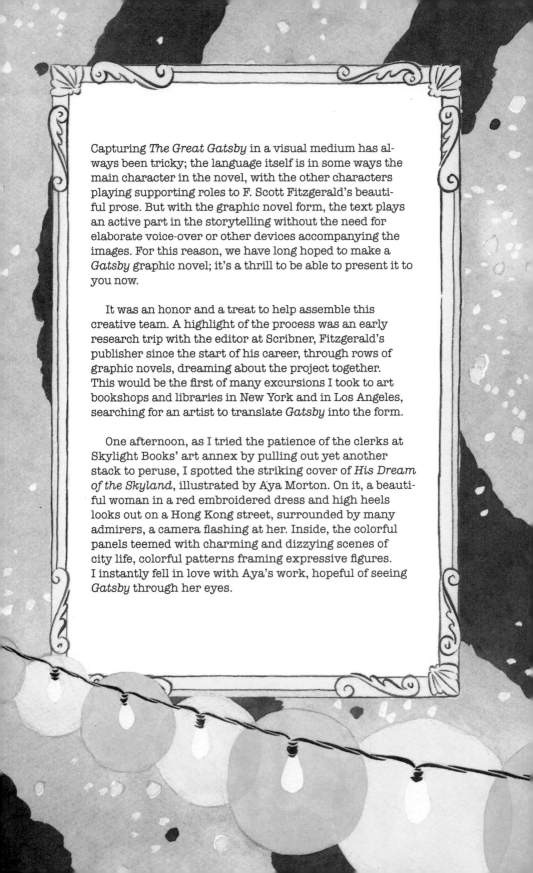

Capturing *The Great Gatsby* in a visual medium has always been tricky; the language itself is in some ways the main character in the novel, with the other characters playing supporting roles to F. Scott Fitzgerald's beautiful prose. But with the graphic novel form, the text plays an active part in the storytelling without the need for elaborate voice-over or other devices accompanying the images. For this reason, we have long hoped to make a *Gatsby* graphic novel; it's a thrill to be able to present it to you now.

It was an honor and a treat to help assemble this creative team. A highlight of the process was an early research trip with the editor at Scribner, Fitzgerald's publisher since the start of his career, through rows of graphic novels, dreaming about the project together. This would be the first of many excursions I took to art bookshops and libraries in New York and in Los Angeles, searching for an artist to translate *Gatsby* into the form.

One afternoon, as I tried the patience of the clerks at Skylight Books' art annex by pulling out yet another stack to peruse, I spotted the striking cover of *His Dream of the Skyland*, illustrated by Aya Morton. On it, a beautiful woman in a red embroidered dress and high heels looks out on a Hong Kong street, surrounded by many admirers, a camera flashing at her. Inside, the colorful panels teemed with charming and dizzying scenes of city life, colorful patterns framing expressive figures. I instantly fell in love with Aya's work, hopeful of seeing *Gatsby* through her eyes.

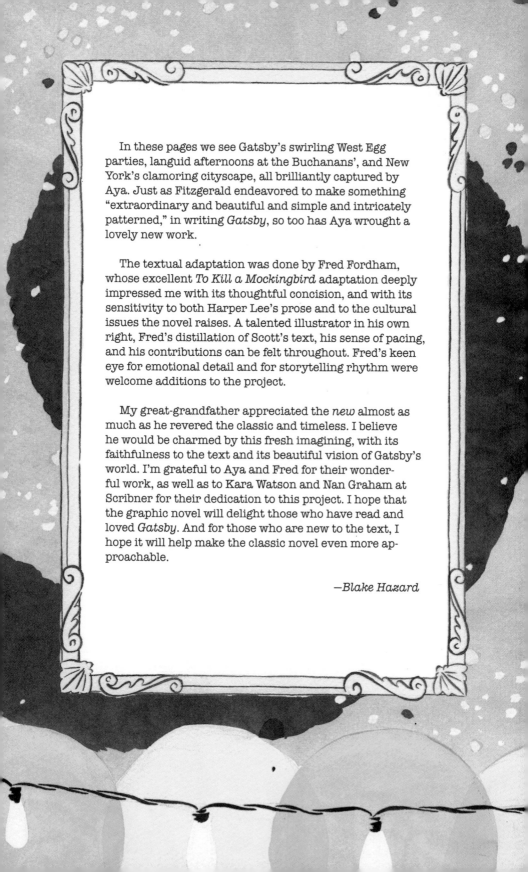

In these pages we see Gatsby's swirling West Egg parties, languid afternoons at the Buchanans', and New York's clamoring cityscape, all brilliantly captured by Aya. Just as Fitzgerald endeavored to make something "extraordinary and beautiful and simple and intricately patterned," in writing *Gatsby*, so too has Aya wrought a lovely new work.

The textual adaptation was done by Fred Fordham, whose excellent *To Kill a Mockingbird* adaptation deeply impressed me with its thoughtful concision, and with its sensitivity to both Harper Lee's prose and to the cultural issues the novel raises. A talented illustrator in his own right, Fred's distillation of Scott's text, his sense of pacing, and his contributions can be felt throughout. Fred's keen eye for emotional detail and for storytelling rhythm were welcome additions to the project.

My great-grandfather appreciated the *new* almost as much as he revered the classic and timeless. I believe he would be charmed by this fresh imagining, with its faithfulness to the text and its beautiful vision of Gatsby's world. I'm grateful to Aya and Fred for their wonderful work, as well as to Kara Watson and Nan Graham at Scribner for their dedication to this project. I hope that the graphic novel will delight those who have read and loved *Gatsby*. And for those who are new to the text, I hope it will help make the classic novel even more approachable.

—*Blake Hazard*

Then wear the gold hat, if that will move her;
  If you can bounce high, bounce for her too,
Till she cry "Lover, gold-hatted, high-bouncing lover,
  I must have you!"

—*Thomas Parke D'Invilliers*

ONCE AGAIN
TO
ZELDA

CHAPTER
I

In my younger and more vulnerable years my father gave me some advice that I've been turning over in my mind ever since.

PENNSYLVANIA STATION

"Whenever you feel like criticizing anyone," he told me, "just remember that all the people in this world haven't had the advantages that you've had."

Reserving judgments is a matter of infinite hope.

I am still a little afraid of missing something if I forget that, as my father snobbishly suggested, and I snobbishly repeat, a sense of the fundamental decencies is parceled out unequally at birth.

And, after boasting this way of my tolerance, I come to the admission that it has a limit.

When I came back from the East last autumn I felt that I wanted the world to be in uniform and at a sort of moral attention forever.

I wanted no more riotous excursions with privileged glimpses into the human heart.

Only Gatsby was exempt from my reaction.

Gatsby, who represented everything for which I have an unaffected scorn.

If personality is an unbroken series of successful gestures, then there was something gorgeous about him, some heightened sensitivity to the promises of life . . .

As if he were related to one of those intricate machines that register earthquakes ten thousand miles away.

It was an extraordinary gift for hope, a romantic readiness such as I have never found in any other person and which it is not likely I shall ever find again.

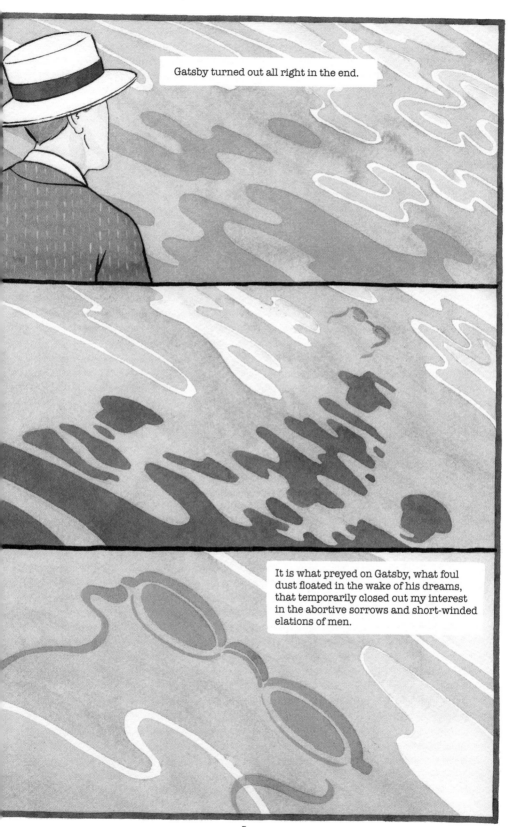

I graduated from New Haven in 1915, and a little later I participated in that delayed Teutonic migration known as the Great War. I enjoyed the counterraid so throroughly that I came back restless.

Instead of being the warm center of the world, the Middle West now seemed like the ragged edge of the universe. So I decided to go East and learn the bond business.

It was a matter of chance that I should have rented a house in one of the strangest communities in North America.

Everyone I knew was in the bond business, so I supposed it could support one more single man.

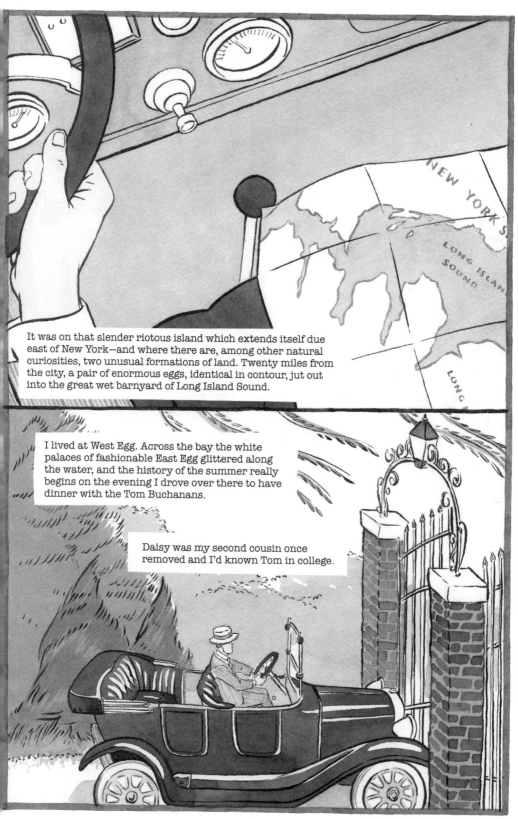

It was on that slender riotous island which extends itself due east of New York—and where there are, among other natural curiosities, two unusual formations of land. Twenty miles from the city, a pair of enormous eggs, identical in contour, jut out into the great wet barnyard of Long Island Sound.

I lived at West Egg. Across the bay the white palaces of fashionable East Egg glittered along the water, and the history of the summer really begins on the evening I drove over there to have dinner with the Tom Buchanans.

Daisy was my second cousin once removed and I'd known Tom in college.

And so it happened that on that warm, windy evening I went to see two old friends whom I scarcely knew at all.

Tom had changed since his New Haven years.

8

11

14

16

18

19

22

26

30

It seemed to me that the thing for Daisy to do was to rush out of the house, child in arms—but apparently there were no such intentions in her head.

As for Tom, the fact that he "had some woman in New York" was really less surprising than that he had been depressed by a book.

It was Mr. Gatsby himself, come out to determine what share was his of our local heavens.

I decided to call to him. Miss Baker had mentioned him at dinner, and that would do for an introduction.

But I didn't call to him, for he gave a sudden intimation that he was content to be alone—he stretched out his arms toward the dark water in a curious way, and far as I was from him I could have sworn he was trembling.

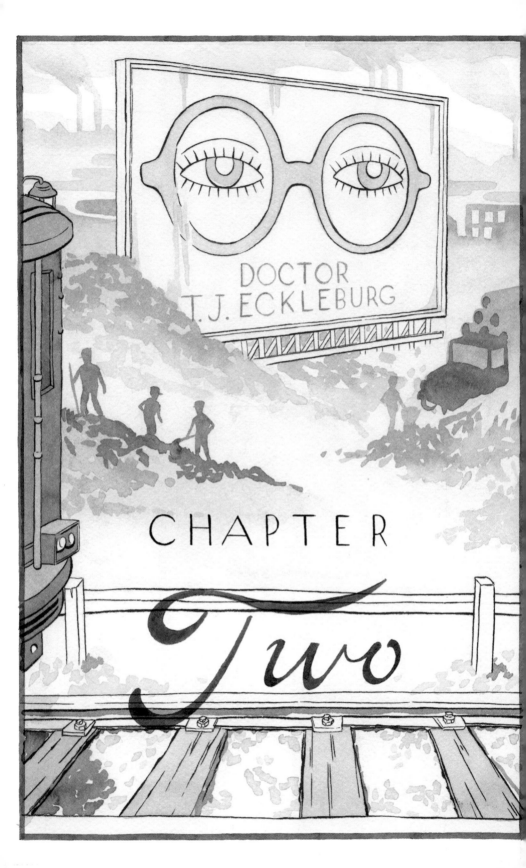

38

39

40

You don't say. Well, that's—

My dear, most of these fellas will cheat you every time.

Mrs. Wilson had changed her costume sometime before, and with the influence of the new dress her personality had also undergone a change.

All they think of is money.

The intense vitality that had been so remarkable in the garage was converted into impressive hauteur.

I had a woman up here last week to look at my feet, and when she gave me the bill you'd of thought she had my appendicitus out.

What was the name of the woman?

Mrs. Eberhardt. She goes around looking at people's feet in their own homes.

I like your dress.

45

47

I wanted to get out and walk eastward toward the Park through the soft twilight, but each time I tried to go I became entangled in some wild, strident argument which pulled me back, as if with ropes, into my chair.

Yet high over the city our line of yellow windows must have contributed their share of human secrecy to the casual watcher in the darkening streets . . .

And I was him, too, looking up and wondering.

I was within and without, simultaneously enchanted and repelled by the inexhaustible variety of life.

Sometime toward midnight Tom Buchanan and Mrs. Wilson stood face-to-face discussing, in impassioned voices, whether Mrs. Wilson had any right to mention Daisy's name.

Daisy! Daisy! Daisy! I'll say it whenever I want to! Daisy! Dai~

Chapter 3

I believe that on the first night I went to Gatsby's house I was one of the few guests who had actually been invited.

People were not invited—they went there.

Dear Mr. Carraway,

The honor would be entirely mine if you would attend my little party tonight. I had intended to call on you long before, but a peculiar combination of circumstances prevented it.

Yours,

Jay Gatsby

I arrived a little after seven, and wandered around rather ill at ease among the swirls and eddies of people I didn't know.

The two or three other people of whom I asked Gatsby's whereabouts denied so vehemently any knowledge of his movements that I slunk off in the direction of the cocktail table.

I was on my way to get roaring drunk from sheer embarrassment when Jordan Baker came out of the house.

Welcome or not, I found it necessary to attach myself to someone before I should begin to address cordial remarks to the passersby.

Hello!

My voice seemed unnaturally loud across the garden.

I thought you might be here.

I remembered you lived next door to~

Hello!

Sorry you didn't win.

You don't know who we are but we met you here a month ago.

59

Let's find our host.

The bar, where we glanced first, was crowded, but Gatsby was not there. She couldn't find him from the top of the steps, and he wasn't on the veranda.

On a chance we tried an important-looking door, and walked into a high Gothic library, paneled with carved English oak, and probably transported complete from some ruin overseas.

63

Your face is familiar~

Weren't you in the Third Division during the war?

Why, yes. I was in the Ninth Machine-Gun Battalion.

I was in the Seventh Infantry until June nineteen-eighteen. I knew I'd seen you somewhere before.

We talked for a moment about some wet, gray little villages in France. Evidently he lived in this vicinity, for he told me that he had just bought a hydroplane, and was going to try it out in the morning.

Want to go with me, old sport?

What time?

Any time that suits you best.

This is an unusual party for me. I haven't even seen the host. I live over there~

And this man Gatsby sent over his chauffeur with an invitation.

His was one of those rare smiles with a quality of eternal reassurance in it, that you might come across four or five times in your life.

It faced—or seemed to face—the whole external world for an instant, and then concentrated on you with an irresistible prejudice in your favor.

65

I had expected Gatsby would be a florid and corpulent person in his middle years.

Who is he? Do you know?

He's just a man named Gatsby.

Where is he from, I mean? And what does he do?

He told me once he was an Oxford man.

However, I don't believe it.

Why not?

I don't know. I just don't think he went there.

Something in her tone reminded me of the other girl's "I think he killed a man."

Anyhow, he gives large parties. And I like large parties. They're so intimate.

At small parties there isn't any privacy.

Ladies and gentlemen!

At the request of Mr. Gatsby, we are going to play for you Mr. Vladimir Tostoff's latest work.

If you read the newspapers, you know it caused a big sensation . . .

Some sensation.

Miss Baker? I beg your pardon, but Mr. Gatsby would like to speak to you alone.

I was alone and it was almost two.

For some time confused and intriguing sounds had issued from a room which overhung the terrace. I went inside.

The singer had drunk a quantity of champagne, and during the course of her song she had decided, ineptly, that everything was very, very sad.

She had a fight with a man who says he's her husband.

A sudden emptiness seemed to flow now from the windows and the great doors, endowing with complete isolation the figure of the host . . .

. . . Who stood on the porch, his hand raised in a formal gesture of farewell.

For a while I lost sight of Jordan Baker, and then in midsummer I found her again.

At first I was flattered to go places with her, because she was a golf champion, and everyone knew her name.

I wasn't actually in love, but I felt a sort of tender curiosity.

The bored, haughty face that she turned to the world concealed something.

Most affectations conceal something eventually, even though they don't in the beginning—and one day I found what it was.

When we were on a house party together up in Warwick, she left a borrowed car out in the rain with the top down, and then lied about it.

And at her first big golf tournament there was a row that nearly reached the newspapers—a suggestion that she had moved her ball from a bad lie in the semifinal round. The thing approached the proportions of a scandal—then died away.

She was incurably dishonest, and wasn't able to endure being at a disadvantage.

It made no difference to me.

It was on that same house party that we had a curious conversation about driving a car.

You're a rotten driver.

You ought to be more careful.

I am careful.

No, you're not.

Well, other people are. It takes two to make an accident.

Suppose you meet someone just as careless as yourself?

I hope I never will. I hate careless people.

That's why I like you.

Her gray, sun-strained eyes stared straight ahead, but she had deliberately shifted our relations, and for a moment I thought I loved her.

But I am slow-thinking and full of interior rules that act as brakes on my desires, and I knew that first I had to get myself definitely out of that tangle back home.

I'd been writing letters once a week and signing them: "Love, Nick."

Everyone suspects himself of at least one of the cardinal virtues, and this is mine: I am one of the few honest people that I have ever known.

I had talked with Gatsby perhaps half a dozen times in the past month and found, to my disappointment, that he had little to say.

Good morning, old sport. You're having lunch with me today and I thought we'd ride up together.

So my first impression, that he was a person of some undefined consequence, had gradually faded and he had become simply the proprietor of an elaborate roadhouse next door.

And then came that disconcerting ride.

Look here, old sport. What's your opinion of me, anyhow?

A little overwhelmed, I began the generalized evasions which that question deserves.

"Paris, Venice, Rome~collecting jewels, chiefly rubies, hunting big game, painting a little, things for myself only..."

"Trying to forget something very sad that had happened to me long ago."

With an effort I managed to restrain my incredulous laughter. The very phrases were worn so threadbare that they evoked no image except that of a turbaned "character" leaking sawdust at every pore as he pursued a tiger through the Bois de Boulogne.

Then came the war, old sport.

It was a great relief, and I tried very hard to die, but I seemed to bear an enchanted life.

I was promoted to be a major, and every Allied government gave me a decoration~even Montenegro, little Montenegro down on the Adriatic Sea!

Little Montenegro! He lifted up the words and nodded at them—with his smile.

The city seen from the Queensboro Bridge is always the city seen for the first time, in its first wild promise of all the mystery and the beauty in the world.

"Anything can happen now that we've slid over this bridge," I thought; "anything at all . . ."

Even Gatsby could happen, without any particular wonder.

I can't forget so long as I live the night they shot Rosy Rosenthal there. It was six of us at the table, and Rosy had eat and drunk a lot all evening.

When it was almost morning the waiter came up to him with a funny look and says somebody wants to speak to him outside. "All right," says Rosy, and begins to get up, and I pulled him down in his chair.

"Let the bastards come in here if they want you, Rosy, but don't you, so help me, move outside this room."

Did he go?

Sure he went.

He turned around in the door and said: "Don't let that waiter take away my coffee!" Then he went out on the sidewalk, and they shot him three times in his full belly and drove away.

Excuse me a moment, old sport.

He has to telephone.

Fine fellow, isn't he? Handsome to look at and a perfect gentleman.

Yes.

Have you known Gatsby for a long time?

Several years. I made the pleasure of his acquaintance just after the war. But I knew I had discovered a man of fine breeding after I talked with him an hour.

83

"The largest of the lawns belonged to Daisy Fay's house. She was just eighteen, two years older than me, and by far the most popular of all the young girls in Louisville."

One October day in nineteen-seventeen~

(said Jordan Baker that afternoon, in the tea garden at the Plaza Hotel)

I was walking along from one place to another, half on the sidewalks and half on the lawns . . .

"When I came opposite her house that morning her white roadster was beside the curb, and she was sitting in it with a lieutenant I had never seen before."

"'Hello, Jordan,' she called unexpectedly. 'Please come here.'"

"I was flattered that she wanted to speak to me, because of all the older girls I admired her most."

Are you going to the Red Cross to make bandages?

"I was."

Well then, would you tell them that I can't come today?

"The officer looked at Daisy while she was speaking, in a way that every young girl wants to be looked at sometime, and because it seemed romantic to me I have remembered the incident ever since."

"His name was Jay Gatsby, and I didn't lay eyes on him again for over four years."

By the next year I had a few beaux myself, and I began to play in tournaments, so I didn't see Daisy very often. She went with a slightly older crowd~when she went with anyone at all.

Wild rumors were circulating about her~how her mother had found her packing her bag one winter night to go to New York and say goodbye to a soldier who was going overseas.

"She was effectually prevented, but she wasn't on speaking terms with her family for several weeks . . ."

"She began to cry—she cried and cried. I rushed out and found her mother's maid, and we locked the door and got her into a cold bath."

"She wouldn't let go of the letter."

"We gave her spirits of ammonia and put ice on her forehead and hooked her back into her dress."

"Half an hour later, when we walked out of the room, the pearls were around her neck and the incident was over."

"Next day at five o'clock she married Tom Buchanan without so much as a shiver."

Chapter FIVE

When I came home to West Egg that night I was afraid for a moment that my house was on fire.

Two o'clock and the whole corner of the peninsula was blazing with light.

But there wasn't a sound.

Your place looks like the World's Fair.

Does it?

I have been glancing into some of the rooms.

Let's go to Coney Island, old sport. In my car.

It's too late.

"Well, suppose we take a plunge in the swimming pool? I haven't made use of it all summer."

"I've got to go to bed."

95

It happens to be a rather confidential sort of thing.

I realize now that under different circumstances that conversation might have been one of the crises of my life. But, because the offer was obviously and tactlessly for a service to be rendered, I had no choice except to cut him off there.

I've got my hands full. I'm much obliged but I couldn't take on any more work.

The evening had made me light-headed and happy; I think I walked into a deep sleep as I entered my front door. So I don't know whether or not Gatsby went to Coney Island, or for how many hours he "glanced into rooms" while his house blazed gaudily on.

I called up Daisy from the office next morning, and invited her to come to tea.

Don't bring Tom.

What?

Don't bring Tom.

Who's Tom?

One of the papers said they thought the rain would stop about four.

I think it was *The Journal.*

Have you got everything you need in the shape of— of tea?

I went out the back way and ran for a huge black knotted tree, whose massed leaves made a fabric against the rain.

There was nothing to look at from under the tree except Gatsby's enormous house, so I stared at it, like Kant at his church steeple.

A brewer had built it early in the "period" craze, a decade before, and there was a story that he'd agreed to pay five years' taxes on all the neighboring cottages if the owners would have their roofs thatched with straw. Perhaps their refusal took the heart out of his plan to Found a Family—he went into an immediate decline.

PFFTT

Americans, while occasionally willing to be serfs, have always been obstinate about being peasantry.

After half an hour I went in—after making every possible noise in the kitchen, short of pushing over the stove.

But I don't believe they heard a sound.

...

It's stopped raining.

Has it?

What do you think of that? It's stopped raining.

I'm glad, Jay.

I want you and Daisy to come over to my house.

I'd like to show her around.

You're sure you want me to come?

Absolutely, old sport.

As we wandered through Marie Antoinette music rooms and Restoration salons, I felt that there were guests concealed behind every couch and table, under orders to be breathlessly silent until we had passed through.

107

108

I tried to go then but they wouldn't hear of it; perhaps my presence made them feel more satisfactorily alone.

I know what we'll do. We'll have Klipspringer play the piano.

In the music room Gatsby turned on a solitary lamp beside the piano. He lit Daisy's cigarette from a trembling match, and sat down with her on a couch far across the room, where there was no light save what the gleaming floor bounced in from the hall.

TUOLOMEE

James Gatz of
North Dakota.

Chapter
6

Cody was fifty years old then, a product of the Nevada silver fields, of the Yukon, of every rush for metal since seventy-five. The transactions in Montana copper that made him many times a millionaire found him physically robust but on the verge of soft-mindedness.

A few days later he took Gatsby to Duluth and bought him a blue coat, six pair of white duck trousers, and a yachting cap. And when the *Tuolomee* left for the West Indies and the Barbary Coast, Gatsby left too.

He was employed in a vague personal capacity—while he remained with Cody he was in turn steward, mate, skipper, secretary, and even jailor, for Dan Cody sober knew what lavish doings Dan Cody drunk might soon be about, and he provided for such contingencies by reposing more and more trust in Gatsby.

I remember the portrait of him up in Gatsby's bedroom, a gray, florid man with a hard, empty face—the pioneer debauchee, who during one phase of American life brought back to the Eastern seaboard the savage violence of the frontier brothel and saloon.

And it was from Cody that he inherited money—a legacy of twenty-five thousand dollars. He didn't get it. He never understood the legal device that was used against him, but what remained of the millions went intact to Ella Kaye.

He told me all this very much later, but I've put it down here with the idea of exploding those first wild rumors about his antecedents, which weren't even faintly true. Moreover, he told it to me at a time of confusion, when I had reached the point of believing everything and nothing about him.

So I take advantage of this short halt, while Gatsby, so to speak, caught his breath, to clear this set of misconceptions away.

For several weeks I didn't see him or hear his voice on the phone—mostly I was in New York, trotting around with Jordan and trying to ingratiate myself with her senile aunt—but finally I went over to his house one Sunday afternoon.

Tom was evidently perturbed at Daisy's running around alone, for on the following Saturday night he came with her to Gatsby's party.

Her glance left me and sought the lighted top of the steps. After all, in the very casualness of Gatsby's party there were romantic possibilities totally absent from her world. What was it up there in the song that seemed to be calling her back inside?

Perhaps some unbelievable guest would arrive, a person infinitely rare and to be marveled at, some authentically radiant young girl who with one fresh glance at Gatsby, one moment of magical encounter, would blot out those five years of unwavering devotion.

Out of the corner of his eye Gatsby saw that the blocks of the sidewalk really formed a ladder and mounted to a secret place above the trees.

Then he
kissed her.

It was when curiosity about Gatsby was at its highest that the lights in his house failed to go on one Saturday night—and, as obscurely as it had begun, his career as Trimalchio was over.

I wanted people who wouldn't gossip. Daisy comes over quite often—in the afternoons.

They're some people Wolfshiem wanted to do something for. They're all brothers and sisters. They used to run a small hotel.

I see.

He dismissed every servant in his house, replacing them with half a dozen others who never went into West Egg Village to be bribed by the tradesmen, but ordered moderate supplies over the telephone.

He was calling up at Daisy's request—would I come to lunch at her house tomorrow? Miss Baker would be there.

Half an hour later Daisy herself telephoned and seemed relieved to find that I was coming.

Something was up.

137

139

145

146

He had discovered that Myrtle had some sort of life apart from him in another world, and the shock had made him physically sick. I stared at him and then at Tom, who had made a parallel discovery less than an hour before . . .

And it occurred to me that there was no difference between men, in intelligence or race, so profound as the difference between the sick and the well.

I'll let you have that car. I'll send it over tomorrow.

Over the ash heaps the giant eyes of Doctor T. J. Eckleburg kept their vigil, but I perceived, after a moment, that other eyes were regarding us with peculiar intensity from less than twenty feet away.

So engrossed was she that she had no consciousness of being observed, and one emotion after another crept into her face like objects into a slowly developing picture.

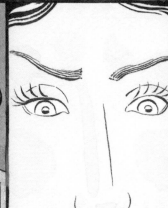

Her expression was one I had often seen on women's faces, but on Myrtle Wilson's face it seemed purposeless and inexplicable . . .

Until I realized that her eyes, wide with jealous terror, were fixed not on Tom . . .

But on Jordan Baker, whom she took to be his wife.

There is no confusion like the confusion of a simple mind, and as we drove away Tom was feeling the hot whips of panic.

His wife and his mistress, until an hour ago secure and inviolate, were slipping precipitately from his control.

Instinct made him step on the accelerator with the double purpose of overtaking Daisy and leaving Wilson behind, and we sped along toward Astoria at fifty miles an hour, until, among the spidery girders of the elevated, we came in sight of the easygoing blue coupé.

Where are we going?

It's so hot. You go. We'll ride around and meet you after.

How about the movies?

We'll meet you on some corner. I'll be the man smoking two cigarettes.

Instead, we all took the less explicable step of engaging the parlor of a suite in the Plaza Hotel. The notion originated with Daisy's suggestion that we hire five bathrooms and take cold baths, and then assumed more tangible form as "a place to have a mint julep."

Open another window!

There aren't any more.

148

149

150

153

155

157

158

They were gone, without a word, snapped out, made accidental, isolated, like ghosts, even from our pity.

Want any of this stuff? Jordan? ... Nick?

Nick?

No...

I just remembered that today's my birthday.

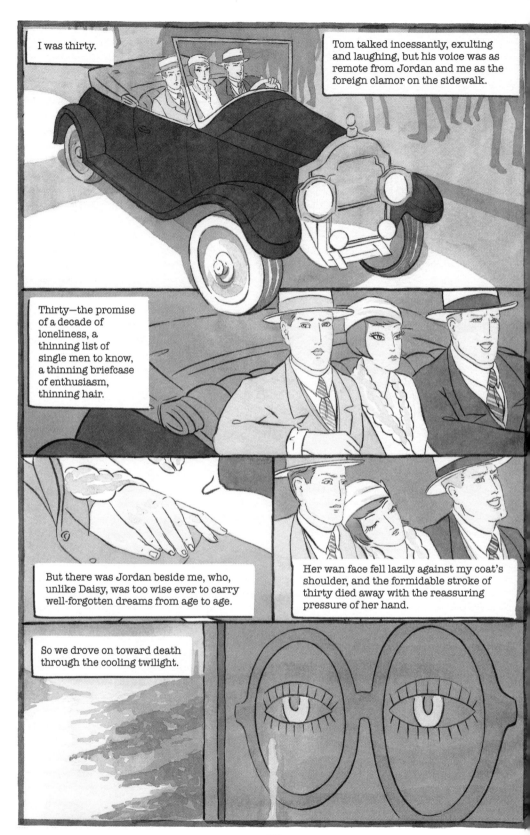

I was thirty.

Tom talked incessantly, exulting and laughing, but his voice was as remote from Jordan and me as the foreign clamor on the sidewalk.

Thirty—the promise of a decade of loneliness, a thinning list of single men to know, a thinning briefcase of enthusiasm, thinning hair.

But there was Jordan beside me, who, unlike Daisy, was too wise ever to carry well-forgotten dreams from age to age.

Her wan face fell lazily against my coat's shoulder, and the formidable stroke of thirty died away with the reassuring pressure of her hand.

So we drove on toward death through the cooling twilight.

165

Daisy's home.

I'll telephone for a taxi to take you home, and while you're waiting you and Jordan better go in the kitchen and have them get you some supper—if you want any.

No, thanks. But I'd be glad if you'd order me the taxi. I'll wait outside.

I'd be damned if I'd go in; I'd had enough of all of them for one day.

169

170

A new point of view occurred to me. Suppose Tom found out that Daisy had been driving. He might think he saw a connection in it— he might think anything.

You wait here. I'll see if there's any sign of a commotion.

And yet they weren't unhappy either.

They weren't happy.

There was an unmistakable air of natural intimacy about the picture.

Anyone would have said they were conspiring together.

Is it all quiet up there?

Yes, it's all quiet. You'd better come home and get some sleep.

I want to wait here till Daisy goes to bed. Good night, old sport.

So I walked away and left him standing there in the moonlight . . .

Watching over nothing.

CHAPTER

8

174

What was the use of doing great things if I could have a better time telling her what I was going to do?

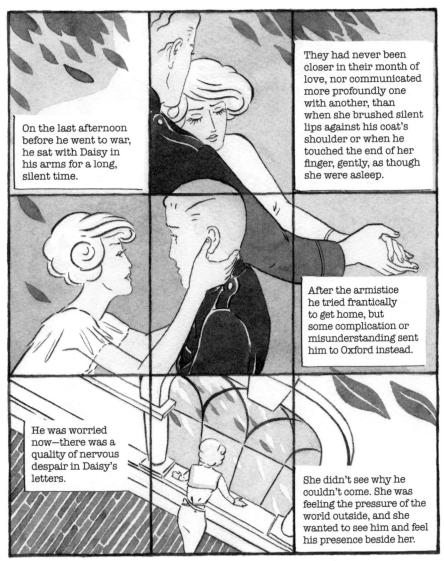

On the last afternoon before he went to war, he sat with Daisy in his arms for a long, silent time.

They had never been closer in their month of love, nor communicated more profoundly one with another, than when she brushed silent lips against his coat's shoulder or when he touched the end of her finger, gently, as though she were asleep.

After the armistice he tried frantically to get home, but some complication or misunderstanding sent him to Oxford instead.

He was worried now—there was a quality of nervous despair in Daisy's letters.

She didn't see why he couldn't come. She was feeling the pressure of the world outside, and she wanted to see him and feel his presence beside her.

Through this twilight universe Daisy began to move again with the season; suddenly she was again keeping half a dozen dates a day with half a dozen men . . .

And drowsing asleep at dawn with the beads and chiffon of an evening dress tangled among dying orchids on the floor beside her bed.

She wanted her life shaped now, immediately—and the decision must be made by some force—of love, of money, of unquestionable practicality—that was close at hand.

That force took shape in the middle of spring with the arrival of Tom Buchanan.

I don't think she ever loved him.

Of course she might have loved him just for a minute, when they were married—and loved me more even then, do you see?

In any case, it was just personal.

He came back from France when Tom and Daisy were still on their wedding trip, and made a miserable but irresistible journey to Louisville on the last of his army pay.

I left feeling that if I'd only searched harder I would have found her. I felt I was leaving her behind . . .

But I was penniless then.

He stayed there a week, walking the streets where their footsteps had clicked together through the November night and revisiting the out-of-the-way places to which they had driven in her white car.

I have an idea that Gatsby himself didn't believe the call from Daisy would come.

If that was true he must have felt that he had lost the old warm world, paid a high price for living too long with a single dream.

He must have looked up at an unfamiliar sky through frightening leaves and shivered as he found what a grotesque thing a rose is and how raw the sunlight was upon the scarcely created grass.

A new world, material without being real, where poor ghosts, breathing dreams like air, drifted fortuitously about . . .

Like that ashen, fantastic figure gliding toward him through the amorphous trees.

CHAPTER

Wilson's movements—he was on foot all the time—were afterward traced to Port Roosevelt and then to Gad's Hill, where he bought a sandwich that he didn't eat, and a cup of coffee. He must have been tired and walking slowly, for he didn't reach Gad's Hill until noon.

Mrs. Buchanan, please.

Left no address? Say when they'd be back?

Then for three hours he disappeared from view. The police, on the strength of his claim that he "had a way of finding out," supposed that he spent that time going from garage to garage thereabouts, inquiring for a yellow car.

Any idea where they are? How I could reach them?

On the other hand, no garage man who had seen him ever came forward, and perhaps he had an easier, surer way of finding out what he wanted to know. By half-past two he was in West Egg, where he asked someone the way to Gatsby's house. So by that time he knew Gatsby's name.

A few days later a Henry C. Gatz, Gatsby's father, arrived from a town in Minnesota.

It was all in the Chicago newspaper. I started right away.

I didn't know how to reach you.

It was a madman. He must have been mad.

HARDLY CAN BELIEVE IT THAT IT IS TRUE AT ALL. SUCH A MAD ACT AS THAT MAN DID SHOULD MAKE US ALL THINK. I CANNOT COME DOWN NOW AS I AM TIED UP IN SOME VERY IMPORTANT BUSINESS AND CANNOT GET MIXED UP IN THIS THING NOW. IF THERE IS ANYTHING I CAN DO A LITTLE LATER LET ME KNOW IN A LETTER BY EDGAR. I HARDLY KNOW WHERE I AM WHEN I HEAR ABOUT A THING LIKE THIS AND AM COMPLETELY KNOCKED DOWN AND OUT.

YOURS TRULY
MEYER WOLFSHIEM

Would you like some coffee?

No, I'm all right now. Where have they got Jimmy?

They were careless people, Tom and Daisy—they smashed up things and creatures and then retreated back into their money or their vast carelessness, or whatever it was that kept them together, and let other people clean up the mess they had made . . .

After Gatsby's death the East was haunted for me. So when the blue smoke of brittle leaves was in the air and the wind blew the wet laundry stiff on the line I decided to come back home.

There was one thing to be done before I left, an awkward, unpleasant thing that perhaps had better have been let alone.

I saw Jordan Baker and talked over and around what had happened to us together, and what had happened afterward to me.

You said a bad driver was only safe until she met another bad driver. Well, I met another bad driver, didn't I?

It was careless of me to make such a wrong guess. I thought you were rather an honest, straightforward person. I thought it was your secret pride.

I'm thirty. I'm five years too old to lie to myself and call it honor.

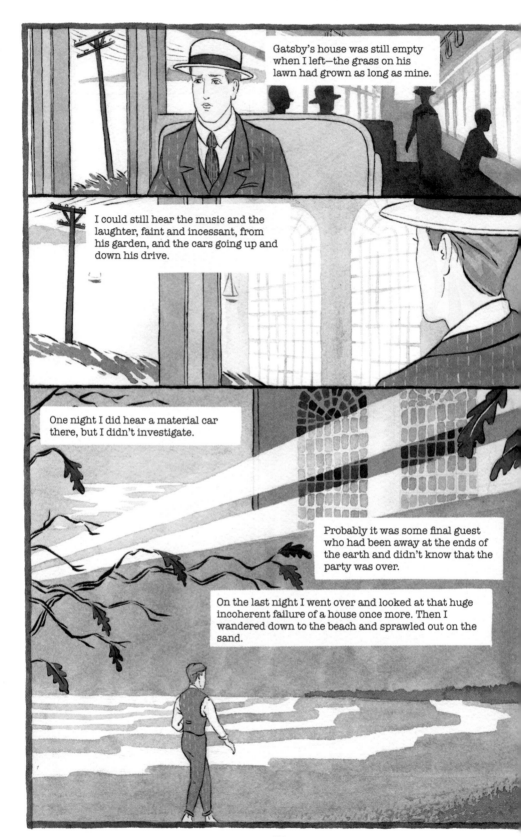

Gatsby's house was still empty when I left—the grass on his lawn had grown as long as mine.

I could still hear the music and the laughter, faint and incessant, from his garden, and the cars going up and down his drive.

One night I did hear a material car there, but I didn't investigate.

Probably it was some final guest who had been away at the ends of the earth and didn't know that the party was over.

On the last night I went over and looked at that huge incoherent failure of a house once more. Then I wandered down to the beach and sprawled out on the sand.

And as the moon rose higher the inessential houses began to melt away until gradually I became aware of the old island here that flowered once for Dutch sailors' eyes—a fresh, green breast of the new world.

Its vanished trees, the trees that had made way for Gatsby's house, had once pandered in whispers to the last and greatest of all human dreams . . .

For a transitory enchanted moment man must have held his breath in the presence of this continent, compelled into an aesthetic contemplation he neither understood nor desired, face-to-face for the last time in history with something commensurate to his capacity for wonder.

And as I sat there brooding on the old, unknown world, I thought of Gatsby's wonder when he first picked out the green light at the end of Daisy's dock.

Gatsby believed in the green light, the orgastic future that year by year recedes before us.